PATRICIA LAUBER

what do
you see

&

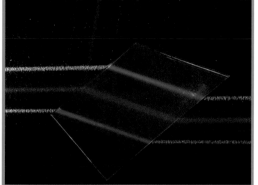

how do
you
see it?

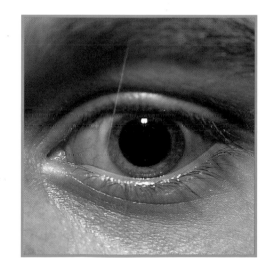

exploring
light, color,
and vision

photographs by
LEONARD LESSIN

Crown Publishers, Inc., New York

Text copyright © 1994 by Patricia G. Lauber

Photograph on page 1 © Blair Seitz/Photo Researchers, Inc. Pages 14 (top left) & 43 (bottom) © Jerome Wexler. Page 16 © Judith Aronson/Peter Arnold, Inc. Page 23 © A.G.E./Peter Arnold, Inc. Page 31 courtesy Keystone View Company. Page 32 (top) © James Martin. Page 34 (top) © Michael Fairchild/Peter Arnold, Inc. Page 34 (bottom) © Matt Meadows/Peter Arnold, Inc. Page 35 © Werner H. Muller/Peter Arnold, Inc. Pages 36 & 46 © Alfred Pasieka/Peter Arnold, Inc. Page 43 (bottom) © Jack R. White. Page 44 courtesy NASA. Page 45 courtesy M. Gallo, D. Willits, R. Lubke, E. Thiede/Alliant Techsystems.

All other photographs copyright © 1994 by Leonard Lessin

Illustrations by Edward Miller

Published by Crown Publishers, Inc., a Random House company, 201 East 50th Street, New York, New York 10022

CROWN is a trademark of Crown Publishers, Inc.

Manufactured in Singapore

Library of Congress Cataloging-in-Publication Data

What do you see? / by Patricia Lauber ;

photographs by Leonard Lessin.

p.   cm.

Includes index.

1. Light—Juvenile literature. 2. Color—Juvenile literature. 3. Vision—Juvenile literature. [1. Light. 2. Vision. 3. Color.]

I. Lessin, Leonard, ill. II. Title.

QC360.L38   1994

535—dc20   93-2388

ISBN 0-517-59390-4 (trade)

0-517-59391-2 (lib. bdg.)

10 9 8 7 6 5 4 3 2 1

First Edition

CONTENTS

LIGHT
AND
SIGHT

You learn about the world through your senses. Mostly you learn about it through your eyes. But seeing takes more than a pair of eyes. It also takes a brain, which works with the eyes. Your eyes send messages to your brain. The brain makes sense of the messages. Then, and only then, do you see what you see.

Your brain and eyes are the parts of your body that make seeing possible. But in order to see, there is still something else you need—light. Everything you look at is seen with light. Without light you see nothing.

Light is one kind of radiation. It is given off, or radiated, by the sun and stars, by fire, by lamps. Anything that radiates light is called a source of light.

A tiny firefly is a source of light, but the moon, no matter how bright, is not. A firefly makes its own light. The moon does not. It shines because the sun's light is bouncing off it, or being reflected.

People, plants, and houses do not usually shine, but they do reflect light. That is why you see them. Rays of light bounce off them and reach your eyes.

But that is only a small part of the story. To find out more about how you see what you see, use your eyes and brain to read on, in a good light.

THE
WAY
LIGHT
MOVES

Shadows can be scary when you don't know what's causing them. They can be fun when you make them yourself. They can be pretty and are good to photograph. They can cool you off on a hot day when you are in the shadow of a tree or a cloud.

Shadows form when light is blocked. They are areas without light. The edge of a shadow forms an outline of whatever is blocking the light—you, your hands, clouds, trees, or other things. This tells you something about the way light travels from one place to another. Light cannot change its own direction and go around things.

Light spreads out from a source in straight lines. When light strikes something, it is reflected and its direction changes. But it is still usually reflected in straight lines. The way light moves is helpful. When you ride a bike, for example, you can be sure that the road is where you see it, because light is reflected from it in straight lines, not in curves and zigzags.

MAKING SHADOWS

You can make a wall show of shadows by using your hands, your body, or solid objects that block rays of light. You will find that the shadows are sharpest when an object is near the wall and there is only one source of light, such as a lamp. But you can also experiment with distance and with the size of the source of light. You can make shadows bigger or smaller. You may even find a way to make some scary ones.

WHEN LIGHT IS REFLECTED

Most of the light that reaches your eyes is reflected light—rays that have bounced off something and kept on moving.

Nearly every surface reflects at least some light. Some smooth, shiny surfaces reflect almost as much light as they receive. They are mirrors.

A wall mirror is a flat, glass mirror. The glass has a silvery coating on the back to make the reflection stronger. When you look in a mirror, it seems as if you are standing behind the glass looking out. Yet what you are seeing is a mirror image of yourself. And that image is not quite the way other people see you.

Touch your right ear and the mirror image touches its left ear. That is, left and right appear reversed in the mirror image. The reason is that light travels in a straight line from your right side to the mirror and is reflected straight back. Your right side appears as the left side of the mirror-you. And that is why you don't look exactly the same in the mirror as you do to other people.

Hold a newspaper up facing the mirror and you will see that the same thing happens. To read the headlines, you have to read backward.

Sometimes you see an ambulance with its front sign written backward. That's not a mistake. Drivers looking in their rearview mirrors see the sign reversed—AMBULANCE—and know to pull out of the way.

You can easily change the direction of light with a small mirror. Hold a pocket mirror so that it catches sunlight streaming in a window. A spot of light will appear on a wall or perhaps the ceiling or floor. It is a reflection from the mirror. By tilting the mirror, you can move the spot around.

In this photograph, a beam of light bounces off a mirror at the bottom of an aquarium. Notice that the light comes from one direction and bounces off the mirror in a different direction. That is, it strikes the mirror at an angle and bounces away at an angle. Light bounces from a flat surface much as a ball bounces from a flat wall. If you throw the ball straight, it comes straight back. If you throw it at a slant, or angle, something else happens. The ball bounces off at an angle, heading in the opposite direction. Light does the same thing.

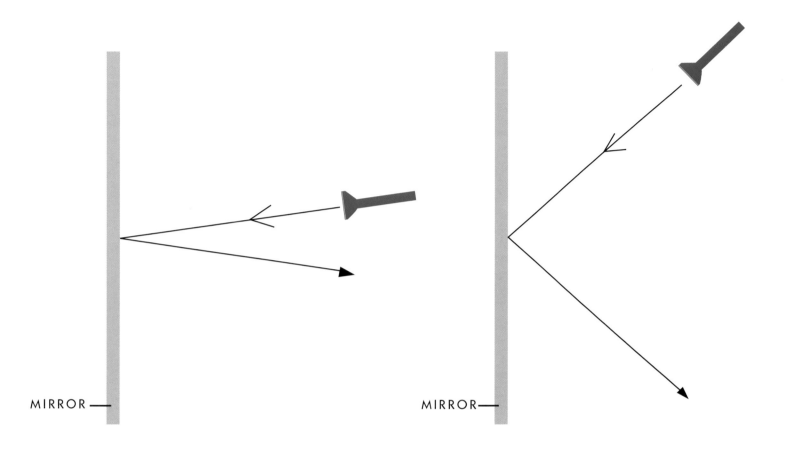

MIRROR ——

MIRROR ——

The two angles are equal. The angle at which light strikes the mirror is the same as the angle at which it bounces away in the opposite direction. Or, as scientists say, the angle of incidence (approach) equals the angle of reflection (departure). This is called the law of reflection.

If you have ever used a toy periscope, then you have also used the law of reflection. What you see at the eyepiece is a reflection that has bounced from angled mirror to angled mirror inside the periscope. The law of reflection also makes mirrors and other reflectors useful in many scientific instruments.

SUPERBOUNCE

Would you like to see a reflection of a reflection of a reflection—a superbounce? All it takes is two mirrors and a small object. Hold the mirrors so that they face each other with the object between them. Then look over the top or to the side of one mirror, into the other. You will see the object over and over again. Would you like to see yourself over and over again? Ask to have a mirror held behind your head next time you get a haircut.

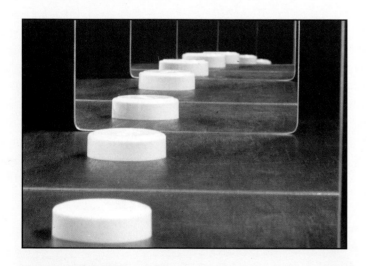

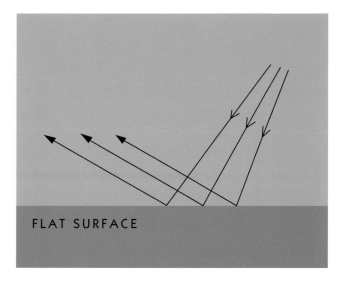

FLAT SURFACE

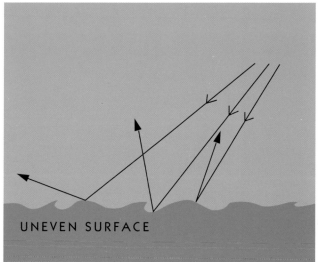

UNEVEN SURFACE

Sometimes you see a building, statue, or tree reflected in still water. The photograph on the left shows a building being reflected by a puddle in the road. The reflection is created by light angling from the building to the puddle, then bouncing up at an equal angle toward your eyes.

If the puddle is rippled (right), it no longer forms a flat mirror. Now rays of light bounce off an uneven surface. With each ray, the angle of incidence still equals the angle of reflection. But the rays strike at various angles, and so they bounce in various directions. They no longer form an image of the building.

A science museum is likely to have some mirrors that are not flat. When you look at yourself, it's like being in a fun house, where mirrors are also curved or wavy. They are designed to make the viewer's image look funny.

Left alone, light moves in straight lines. But by using mirrors, you can change its direction.

If you know how, you can also make light bend.

WHEN LIGHT IS BENT

What has happened to this spoon? The answer is: Nothing—it's simply been put in a glass of water. You are looking at an example of how light can be bent. The bending of light is called refraction.

Light bounces off most materials. It also passes through some. Such materials are called transparent, which means that you can see through them. Air, water, glass, and some plastics are all transparent.

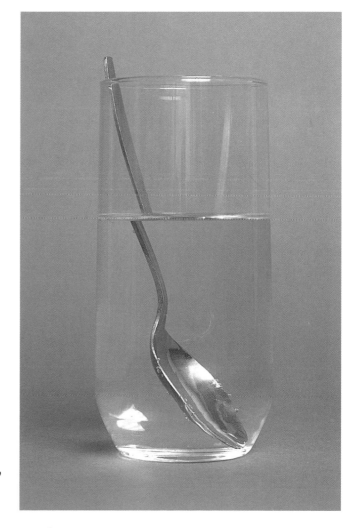

When light passes from one transparent material into another, its speed changes. When light passes from air into water, for example, it slows down. The reason is that water is thicker, or denser, than air—that's why it's harder to wade through water than to walk through air. Glass is denser than water and slows light down even more. As light rays enter denser material, they may also be sharply bent, or refracted.

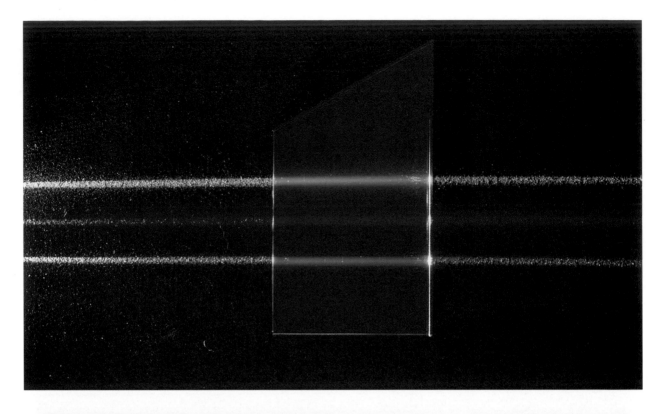

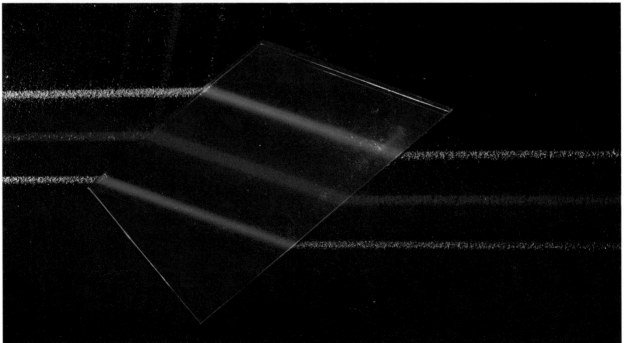

Refraction takes place only if light rays enter the new material at an angle.
If they hit head on, their speed changes, but they are not bent. In the upper
photograph, light rays are hitting the transparent block head on. They pass
through without bending. They hit the transparent block in the lower photograph

at an angle. Some of the light is reflected and bounced up. Most passes through, slowed and bent by the denser material. As the rays pass out of the block, they bend again, speed up, and move in their original direction. Light rays always bend away from the surface when they pass from a less dense material into a denser one.

Light rays bend toward the surface when they pass from denser material into less dense. That is why the pencil seems to be in three parts. Light rays are passing through air, glass, and then air again.

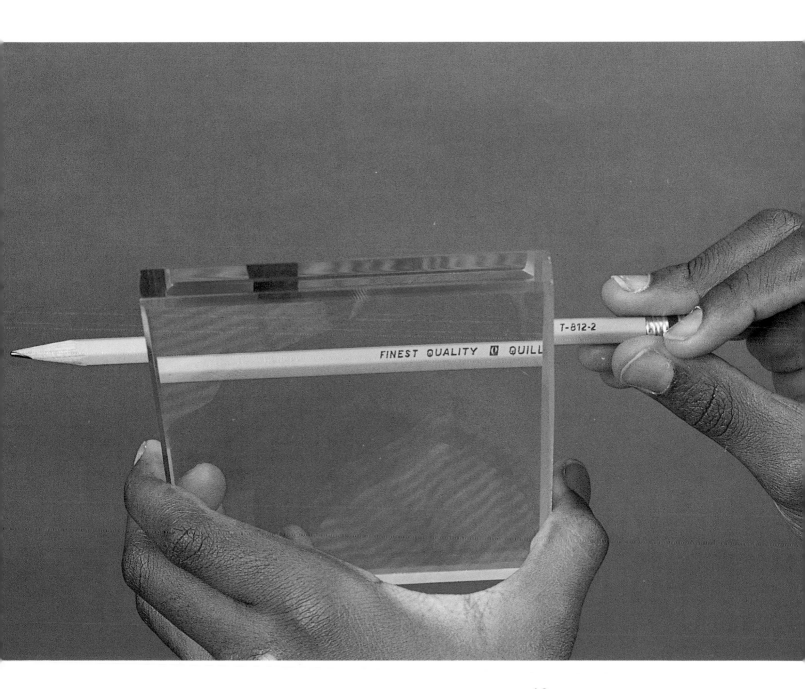

The refraction of light explains many things. It explains, for example, why you may find it hard to pick up something that is under water—if your head is above water, the object may not be where it appears to be. It explains why this toy diver, half out of the water, appears to be in two pieces.

Refraction also explains what happens when light passes through a lens.

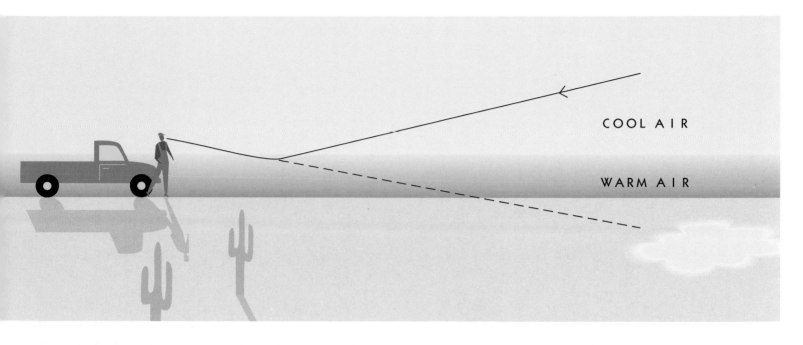

COOL AIR

WARM AIR

MIRAGES

If you are in a car on a hot summer day, you may see what looks like a pool of water shimmering on the road ahead. But when you reach that place, the road is dry. What you have seen is a mirage. It is caused by refraction.

Some of the light rays reflected from the sky are traveling toward the road. They are passing through cool air, which is denser than hot air. As they reach the hot air above the road, they are refracted up to your eyes. They seem to be coming from the road ahead. What appears to be water is really a reflection of sky.

There are many sorts of mirage. But all have the same cause—rays of light are being refracted as they pass from air that is one temperature to air that is a different temperature.

THE REAPPEARING COIN

Here's a way to make a coin vanish, then reappear.

Place a coin near the edge of a pot, pan, or other container that you can't see through. Without moving your head, back away slowly, until you can no longer see the coin. Then stop. Ask a friend to pour water into the container—gently, so as not to move the coin. Suddenly you can see the coin again. Why? Light rays reflected from the coin are being bent toward the surface as they leave water and enter air. (But remember: Light must enter the water at an angle.)

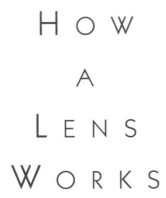

How a Lens Works

When you use a magnifying glass, you are using a lens. When you use a microscope, you are also using one or more lenses. The lenses gather light and send it toward your eye. The lens in a camera sends light toward the film.

A lens is a piece of transparent material that has at least one smoothly curved surface. There are two main kinds of lens.

One kind bulges. It is called a convex lens.

The other kind curves in. It is called a concave lens. You can easily remember which is which. A con*cave* lens looks as if it had *caved* in.

When light rays pass through a lens, they are bent, or refracted.

They are bent inward when they pass through a convex lens.

They are bent outward when they pass through a concave lens.

Most of the lenses you use, such as a magnifying glass, are convex.

When you hold the glass near an object, light rays are reflected from the object through the lens. They are bent in such a way that your eye sees a big image.

When you hold it farther away, something else happens.

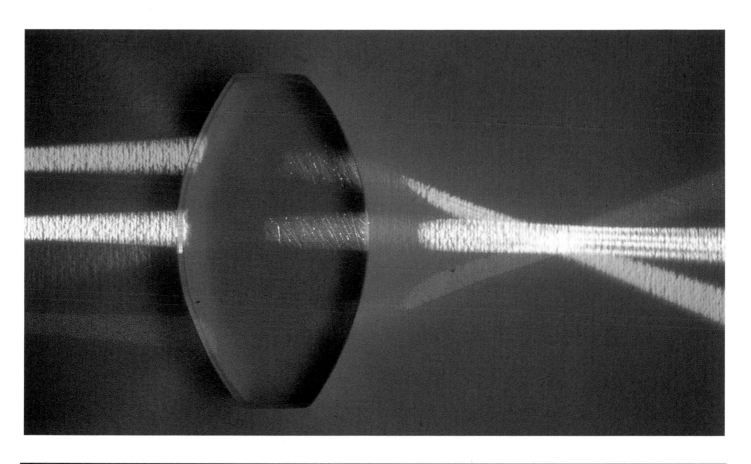

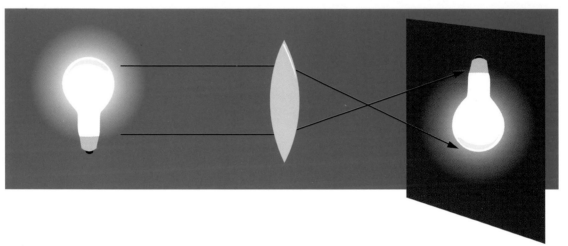

The best way to see what happens is to light a lamp on a table. Prop a piece of cardboard against some books, about 2 feet from the lamp. Hold the magnifying glass between the cardboard and the lamp. Move it slowly back and forth until you see a clear image of the lamp on the cardboard.

The image may surprise you—it's upside down and reversed from left to right. The reason is refraction. Light rays were bent inward as they passed through the lens.

The image that forms on film in a camera is also upside down and reversed. Light rays have passed through a convex lens in the camera.

Light is also refracted when it passes into your eyes. And the image that forms is upside down and reversed.

How the Eye Works

Seeing begins when light enters your eye. Most of it is reflected light, and it brings information with it. The light rays travel through the eye. They form an image on the back wall of the eye, a part called the retina.

The retina is packed with cells that sense light. Some are shaped like cones; they sense color. Some are shaped like rods; they work in dim light and form images in black and white. Each eye has about 130 million rods and cones, all packed into an area the size of a postage stamp.

On its way to the retina, light passes through the cornea and the lens. Both are convex, and so they bend light inward. The image that forms on the retina is upside down and reversed. Because the retina is curved, the image is also curved.

Rods and cones send messages to the brain, along the optic nerve. The brain makes sense of the messages. And you see what you see as it really is—not upside down, reversed, and curved.

The retina has a blind spot, where the optic nerve enters the eye. Here there are no cells that help to form an image. You almost never notice that you have a blind spot. But it's easy to prove that you do.

THE PARTS OF THE EYE

The cornea is a transparent outer covering, which is convex.

Behind the cornea is a clear liquid.

The pupil is the dark spot at the center of the eye. It is an opening into the dark inside of the eye.

The colored part of the eye, around the pupil, is the iris. It is a ring of muscle that changes the size of the pupil.

Behind the pupil is the lens, which is also convex. And behind the lens is a clear jelly.

The retina forms the back wall of the eye.

The optic nerve carries messages to the brain.

THE PUPIL

The size of the pupil changes with the amount of light. It is wider when light is dim, smaller when light is bright. The iris controls the size of the pupil and the amount of light that enters the eye.

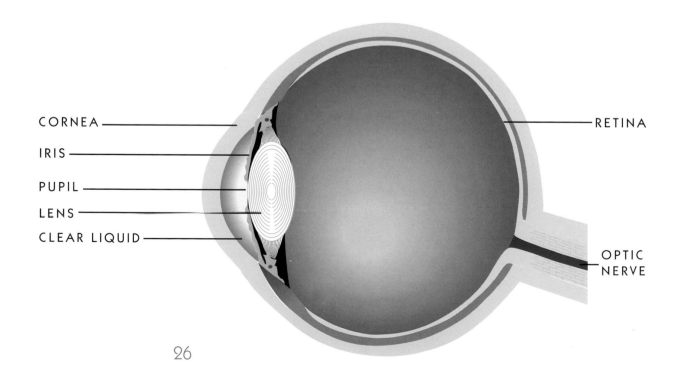

CORNEA ——————— RETINA

IRIS ——

PUPIL ——

LENS ——

CLEAR LIQUID ——

OPTIC NERVE

Hold this book at arm's length. Cover your left eye and use your right eye to look at the baseball in the photograph. Move the book slowly toward you until the tennis ball disappears. Its image is falling on the blind spot in your right eye.

Cover your right eye and use your left to look at the tennis ball. Move the book and the baseball will disappear.

One reason you don't notice a blind spot is that you see with two eyes. One eye usually makes up for the other's blind spot.

With normal eyesight, the image that forms on the retina is sharp and clear, like the image of the lamp when you moved the magnifying glass to the right place. In the eye, the lens does not move. But a muscle squeezes it, making it thicker, when you look at something close up. The muscle relaxes, making the lens thinner, when you look at something far away.

Near-sighted eyes cannot see distant objects clearly because their lenses do not grow thin enough. Sharp images form too soon, before light rays reach the retina. These eyes can be helped by glasses that spread light rays so that they come together on the retina.

With far-sighted eyes, sharp images of nearby objects do not form soon enough. These eyes can be helped by glasses that bring light rays together sooner.

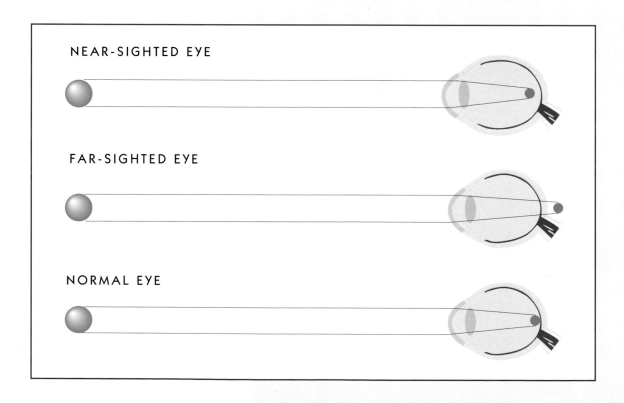

NEAR-SIGHTED EYE

FAR-SIGHTED EYE

NORMAL EYE

Your two eyes work together. They look in the same direction at the same time. Yet they do not see exactly the same thing. The reason is that they are set a small distance apart in your head. Each sees from a slightly different angle, as you can easily prove.

Hold your right hand about 12 inches from your nose. With both eyes open you can see most of the hand.

Close or cover your right eye and you will see most of the palm but little of the knuckles.

Close or cover your left eye and you no longer see the palm, but you do see the knuckles clearly.

Each eye sends a slightly different message to the brain. The brain puts them together and blends them.

Because your eyes work together, you are able to judge distance. And you see that things are not flat—they have depth. It's helpful to see depth—try threading a needle with one eye closed!

Seeing in depth is called stereoscopic vision.

A hundred years ago people amused themselves with a toy called a stereoscope (above left). It held two photographs, taken from slightly different angles. A viewer looked at one photograph with the right eye, at the other with the left. And what the viewer saw was one photograph with depth.

You can try something like this yourself, using the photographs on the facing page and a pocket mirror.

Hold the mirror against the left side of your nose, about 6 inches above the colored dot. Look at the right picture with your right eye. Move the mirror gently until the reflected image of the left-hand picture falls on top of the right one. You now see one picture with depth.

In its own way, the brain takes two images and puts them together.

Charles Lindbergh, who made the first nonstop flight from New York to Paris, with his aircraft, The Spirit of St. Louis.

SEEING DIFFERENT THINGS

A few animals have two eyes that can look in different directions at the same time. The chameleon is one and the sea gull is another. One eye may look straight ahead, while the other looks off to the side. When the animal sees something to eat, both eyes look at it, and the animal can see in depth.

A HOLE IN YOUR HAND?

The brain usually blends information from both eyes smoothly and well. You aren't even aware of what it's doing. But sometimes the eyes send confusing messages to the brain. The brain puts them together and you see something strange, like this:

Roll a sheet of typing paper into a tube that is 11 inches long and about an inch in diameter. Look through the tube with one eye. Keep the other eye open, but block its view by holding your open hand beside the far end of the tube. The palm should be facing you.

After a little while, you will see what your brain does with these two images. It puts them together, and what you see is a hand with a hole in it.

When you look around by day, you see not only in depth but also in color. As daylight fades, you see less and less color. Trees, for example, grow darker and darker, until they are just black shapes. Colors are part of the lighted world. But they may not be exactly what you think they are.

SOME OTHER EYES

Owls are night hunters. Their eyes have far more rods than cones. Some owls can see in light so dim that you cannot see at all. But an owl has few cones and is almost completely color-blind by day. Owls also have huge, saucer-like eyes, which help to gather light.

Cats hunt by both night and day. When they need to see clearly in dim light, their oval pupils open wide. In bright light, the pupils close into narrow slits. Like some other animals, cats have eyes that seem to glow in the dark. Each eye has a mirror-like lining behind the retina. The lining reflects light forward, and the cells that sense light are given a second chance to do so. When this lining reflects light, the eyes appear to glow.

Animals that hunt for food need to judge distance and to see depth. So do animals that spend time in trees. Look at these animals and you see that their eyes are set in the front of their heads. Both eyes see the same thing and the animal sees depth.

Animals that eat plants have a different need. They need to see the animals that hunt them. Their eyes do not both look forward at the same things. But without moving its head, a rabbit can see all around, even in back of itself. A rabbit sees a flat world, without depth. But it does not need to see depth to find food. It does need to see animals that eat rabbits.

C O L O R S
Y O U
S E E

The late afternoon shower ends. The sun comes out. And a rainbow arcs across the sky. Each color—red, orange, yellow, green, blue, and violet—blends smoothly into the next. You cannot tell where one ends and the next begins.

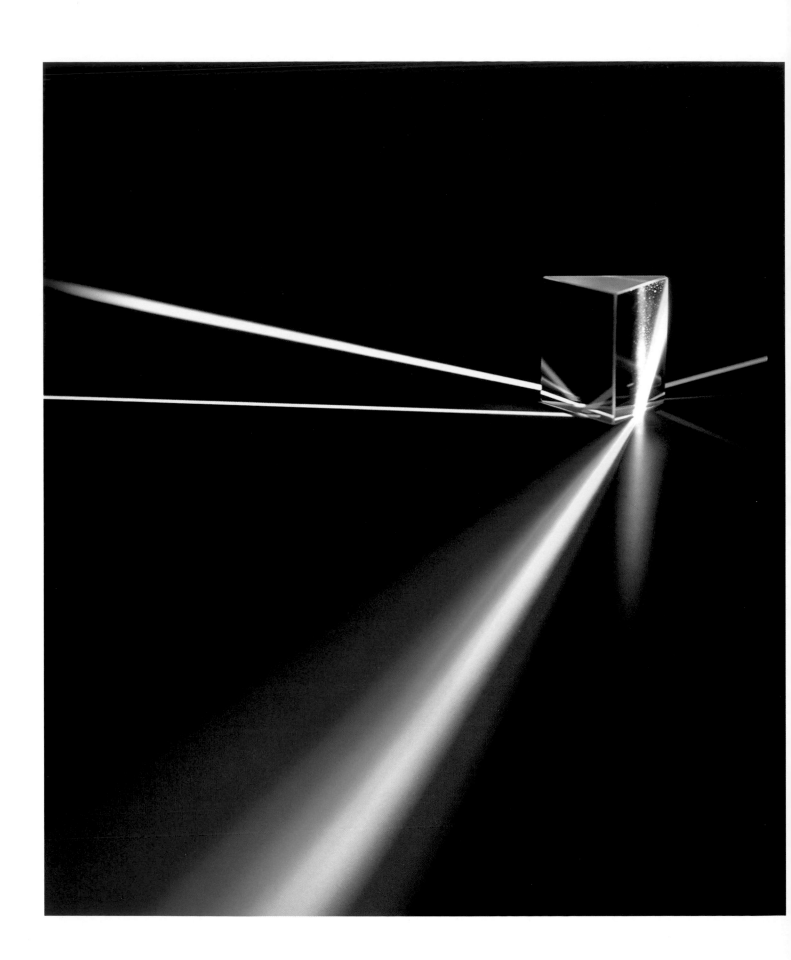

A rainbow seems to come from nowhere. But it really comes from the sun's light. This light is white, and the white light is a mixture of light of many colors.

When a shower ends, tiny drops of water are left in the air. They are shaped like round beads. As sunlight enters the drops, each of its colors is refracted, or bent, by a slightly different amount. And so they are spread out. They are also reflected inside the drops. Their reflections form the rainbow you see.

Sometimes, if the sun is at the right angle, you see a small rainbow in the mist given off by a hose, a lawn sprinkler, an open hydrant, a waterfall. It forms in the same way as a big rainbow in the sky.

You may also see a rainbow at school. Many science rooms have a piece of glass or plastic called a prism. When a ray of sunlight passes through it, the white light becomes a rainbow of color. In science this rainbow band of colors is called a spectrum.

Scientists often speak of light as traveling in waves. And they speak of wavelengths. A wavelength is the distance from the top of one wave to the top of the next.

Every color in the spectrum has its own wavelength. Unlike ocean waves, the colors of the spectrum have very short wavelengths. Violets have the shortest, about 15 millionths of an inch. Reds have the longest, about twice the length of the violets. All the other colors are somewhere in between. These different wavelengths are sensed by our eyes as different colors.

When you look at the world by day, you see that it is full of color—green grass, yellow dandelions, red sweaters, blue mailboxes. Color seems to be part of the things you see. But that is not really so. Light is the only source of color in the world. Without light, grass is not green, dandelions not yellow—nothing has any color. That is why, as daylight fades, color also fades from the natural world. When light disappears, so does color. Color exists only in light.

That may be hard to believe, but it's true.

This is how color works.

When white light falls on grass, the grass reflects only the wavelengths that you see as green. The reason is that grass contains a material called chlorophyll. Chlorophyll takes up, or absorbs, the shortest wavelengths, the violets and blues. It also absorbs the longest, the reds, oranges, yellows. Only the wavelengths of green are not absorbed. They are reflected to your eyes, and so grass appears green.

A dandelion flower contains a material called carotene. Carotene reflects only yellow-orange wavelengths. It absorbs all the rest.

A red sweater has a dye that reflects only red. A blue mailbox has paint that reflects only blue.

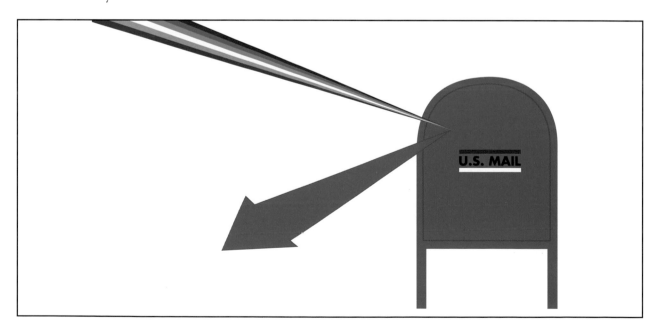

You often see colors that do not appear in the spectrum of white light. Perhaps, for example, you have some black shoes. They have a dye that absorbs all wavelengths and reflects none.

Still other colors are mixtures of spectrum colors. Snow appears white because it reflects all wavelengths—all the wavelengths that together make white. An eggplant appears purple because it reflects red and violet. A brown dog is reflecting yellow, orange, and red.

Mixing spectrum colors is not like mixing paints. A paintbox holds neat squares of colors. Each square is reflecting one or more wavelengths of light and absorbing all the others. Mix all the colors in the paintbox and you get black. The mixture absorbs all wavelengths.

Mix all the colors in the spectrum and you get white.

Mix red and green paint and you get a brown-black. Once again, the paint is absorbing many wavelengths.

Mix red and green light and you get yellow! The reason is that you are mixing long and fairly short wavelengths. Their average falls in the yellow part of the spectrum—and that is reflected to your eyes.

By now you should be able to explain why this apple appears red in daylight but black when seen in yellow light. Think about it before you read on.

The reason is that yellow light contains no red, the only color that the apple can reflect.

In the same way, the tomato in this sandwich seems to disappear when photographed in red light. The white bread has nothing to reflect except red. It becomes the same color as the tomato.

The color you see is the part of the spectrum that is reflected to your eyes. The colors you see are also the ones that your eyes can sense. There are a few others that your eyes cannot see at all.

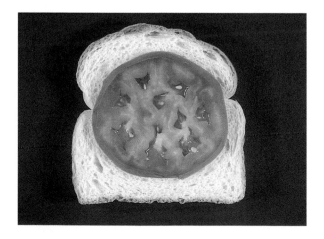 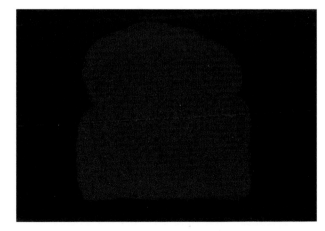

MAN-MADE LIGHT

Man-made light is also made up of different wavelengths. But it is usually not the same as sunlight, which holds equal amounts of all the colors of the spectrum. Fluorescent lights, for example, have less red, more blue, and so much green that photographs taken in this light have a greenish cast. A red sweater (above) does not look as red as it does in daylight (below). Sometimes you see deep yellow lights along a highway or street. They give off two wavelengths in the yellow part of the spectrum. A yellow car appears bright yellow. But red, green, or blue cars absorb the yellow light and have almost nothing to reflect. They appear gray or black.

SEEING
THE
UNSEEABLE

Red has the longest wavelengths your eyes can see. Violet has the shortest. Yet there are both longer and shorter wavelengths of light. Human eyes do not see them, but it is possible to show that they exist.

The longer wavelengths are called infrared, meaning "below red." If you could see in the infrared, you would see color beyond red in every rainbow.

Infrared is given off by hot objects. Hold your hand out toward a hot radiator. Nerve endings in your skin sense the heat, but your eyes do not see the infrared rays. The radiator does not look hot. Hot pavements give off infrared rays. So do the bodies of human beings and all other warm-blooded creatures. But all this radiation is invisible to us.

Infrared is given off most strongly by objects that are hot enough to glow—the sun, flames, electric lights. A light bulb sends out rays that you can see. But its strongest radiation is infrared, which you feel but do not see.

By day, sunlight warms everything on the earth's surface. Some of this heat is radiated back into the atmosphere, both by day and by night. If you could see in the infrared, you would see the landscape glow at night.

Infrared can be shown. One way is to use film that senses infrared.

The photograph above left was taken on a hazy day with ordinary film. The photograph above right was taken with film that sensed the infrared radiation passing through the haze.

Infrared can also be detected without film. The picture below was made with an imaging system that sensed the infrared radiation given off by the boy, the hot water pipe, and the flow of warm water.

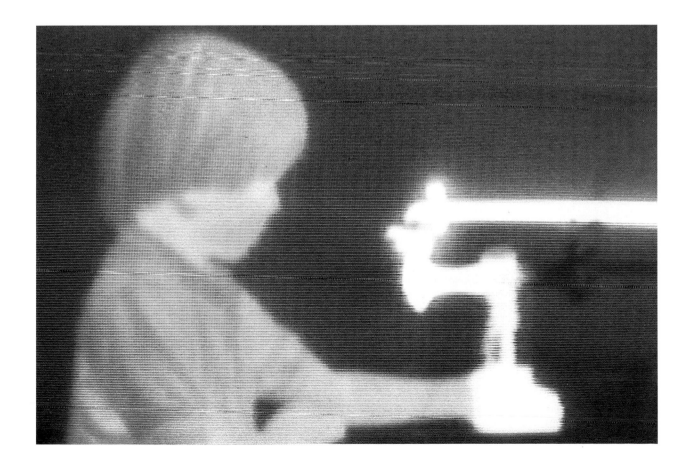

Earth satellites usually carry sensors that can detect infrared as well as wavelengths of visible light. Their findings are recorded and used to make pictures. The pictures tell, as this one does, about the health of crops—by day, healthy green plants reflect infrared strongly, while crops suffering from drought or disease do not.

In making the pictures, scientists use a computer. It gives the infrared reflections a color that human eyes can see. Healthy crops are often shown as bright red, as they are in this picture of the Salton Sea and Imperial Valley in California. Such a picture is called a false-color image. Because farming methods differ in the United States and Mexico, the border appears as a straight line, lower right.

Both the armed forces and police departments need to see in the dark. They use infrared detectors that sense the rays given off by warm bodies and machines. Even better detectors are being developed. They will be smaller, cheaper, and easier to use than the present ones—anybody will be able to own one. One of these detectors was used to find this man slipping silently through the woods at night.

Infrared detectors can be used in many other ways. One is to find where heat leaks out of buildings in winter. The hotter something is, the more infrared it gives off. And so the brightest areas are ones where heat loss is greatest. False color has been added to this picture of a house to show the differences more clearly.

On a summer day the sun's infrared rays heat you up. But they don't give you a sunburn. Sunburns are caused by wavelengths that are shorter than violet. The name for them is ultraviolet, meaning "beyond violet."

Ultraviolet can also be detected. One way of doing this is to capture it on film. The photograph at left shows a black-eyed Susan as it appears to human eyes. The photograph at right shows a pattern of ultraviolet reflections from the same flower. It shows what a bee sees.

Like other insects, a bee can see in the ultraviolet. A honeybee sees patterns in the faces of flowers that humans do not see. The patterns are helpful to the bee. They may mark landing places or pollen or they may guide the bee to nectar.

If you saw like a bee, you would see things that are now invisible to you. But you wouldn't see red, because bees cannot see reflections of red wavelengths. You wouldn't see sharp, clear images either, because a bee's eyes are not made like yours.

If you saw like a bee, the world would be the same, but it would look very different. It would also look very different if you could see in the infrared, yet it would still be the same world.

What do you see? You see the world as it is reflected to your eyes by visible light and made sense of by your brain. And you see it brightened by all the colors of the rainbow.

INDEX